Book Club Edition

First American Edition. Copyright © 1980 by Walt Disney Productions.
All rights reserved under International and Pan-American Copyright
Conventions. Published in the United States by Random House, Inc.,
New York, and simultaneously in Canada by Random House of Canada
Limited, Toronto. Originally published in Denmark as VAKS SOM
REDNINGSMAND by Wangels Forlag A/S Gutenberghus Gruppen
ISBN: 0-394-84741-5 (trade);   0-394-94741-X (lib. bdg.)
Manufactured in the United States of America
    5 6 7 8 9 0   B C D E F G H I J K

WALT DISNEY PRODUCTIONS
presents

SCAMP
to the Rescue

Random House  New York

Jim and his wife Darling live in
a cozy house.

Their dogs Lady and Tramp live
with them.

Lady and Tramp have four
puppies—Fluffy, Ruffy, Scooter,
and Scamp.

Fluffy, Ruffy, and Scooter sleep curled up
in their basket.

It is lined with soft red cloth.

They bark quietly.

They play ball quietly.

And they walk slowly and gracefully.

But Scamp is different.
He jumps off tables.

And he chases after birds.

Sometimes he makes Jim
very angry.

Jim likes Scamp to bring
him his slippers.

But Scamp always runs
away with them instead!

One day Aunt Sara came to visit.
"I would like to take all the puppies
to the park," she said.
"Wonderful!" said Darling.

"Come along!" said Aunt Sara
as they walked to the park.

Fluffy, Ruffy, and Scooter stayed
beside Aunt Sara.

But Scamp ran on ahead.

It was a nice day, and many
people were in the park.

Aunt Sara sat down
on a bench to read.

Fluffy, Ruffy, and Scooter played
quietly beside her.
But Scamp ran off!
"Come back!" shouted Aunt Sara.

Scamp did not stop running. He almost knocked over a man with a cane.

Then he ran through someone's picnic lunch!

Aunt Sara was very angry. "Come here, Scamp!" she cried.

But Scamp kept running.

He ran over to the lily pond
and barked at the ducks and
the frog.
He frightened them away.

Then he dug a hole in the flower garden.

"You bad dog!" shouted Aunt Sara.
She shook her umbrella at him.

"I will take you
home at once."

But Scamp ran away
from Aunt Sara.

She chased him, but
he was faster.

He ran around a bend
and was soon out of sight.

Scamp ran back to where Fluffy, Ruffy, and Scooter were playing.

He hid behind some tall grass, because he wanted to surprise them.

Just then a strange man and woman drove up in a car.

They got out of the car
with a plate of cookies.
"Come have a cookie,
little puppies," they said.

Fluffy, Ruffy,
and Scooter
came closer.

Then the man and woman pulled
out a big bag and popped the
puppies inside!

Scamp watched quietly.

What would happen
next?

The man put the bag in the back of the car.

The bag was tied with a rope, and the puppies were inside.

Aunt Sara had not come back.
When the man and woman drove off,
Scamp chased after them.

The car moved very fast,
but Scamp kept running.

He ran past a fruit stand
on a corner.
Where are they taking
Fluffy, Ruffy, and
Scooter? he wondered.

The man and woman turned the corner.
Scamp ran faster.
He did not want to lose them.

Just then a truck roared around
the corner.

Poor Scamp hurried to get out of the way
and tumbled onto the sidewalk.

Then he rolled right into the fruit
stand!

The fruit went flying in all directions,
and the owner shouted at Scamp.

"You bad dog!" the man said.
He picked up a broom and chased
Scamp away.

When Scamp stopped running, he found
he was in a strange part of town.

He sniffed the ground as he walked along.

He thought he could smell Fluffy, Ruffy,
and Scooter.

Then Scamp came to a large wooden fence.
He did not know what to do next, so he
turned to the right.

Just then he thought he saw the car the
strange man and woman had been driving!

Scamp ran to the corner to get a closer look.

It *was* the car!

It was parked across the street in front of a big house.

Scamp ran across the
street to the fence
around the house.

Fluffy, Ruffy, and
Scooter were behind
the fence.
They looked very sad.

Aunt Sara was still in the park.
She looked everywhere for Scamp.
Then she went back to the bench where
she had left the other puppies.

But they were not there!
"Oh dear!" she cried.

Aunt Sara walked through the park calling for the puppies.

But they did not come running to her as they usually did.

She even looked behind a bush, but only a squirrel was there.

Finally Aunt Sara went home to tell Jim
and Darling that the puppies were lost.

"I looked everywhere for them," Aunt Sara
said sadly.

"We must call the police," said Jim.

Darling began to cry.

Lady and
Tramp were
very worried
about their
puppies.

By this time Scamp had run up to the fence.
Fluffy, Ruffy, and Scooter were so happy
to see him!
Scamp knew how to get them out.
He began to dig a hole under the fence.

Scamp dug and dug.
Dirt was flying in all directions.

Soon he made a deep hole that went
under the fence.

Fluffy crawled under the fence first....

Then came Ruffy.
Scamp barked happily.

Finally Scooter was out, too.

Suddenly the strange man came to the window.

He saw the puppies running away.

"Come back here!" he shouted.

But the puppies
were already far away.

The four puppies ran home.
Scamp led the way.

They raced up the steps of their house,
and Scamp scratched on the door and barked.

Jim opened the door.

He was so happy to see the puppies.

"Thank goodness you are all safe!" he said.

Now the family was back together again.
Somehow Jim, Darling, and Aunt Sara knew
that Scamp had saved the other puppies.
They were very proud of Scamp.

Lady and Tramp were proud of Scamp, too.

They know he is a very special dog, even though he gets into trouble once in a while.